DISNEY · PIXAR

ORIGINS

Storm Chasing

By
Dave Keane

Illustrated by
the Disney Storybook Art Team

Random House 🏠 New York

Materials and characters from the movie *Cars 3*.
Copyright © 2017 Disney Enterprises, Inc. and Pixar. All rights reserved.

Disney/Pixar elements © Disney/Pixar. Published in the United States by Random House Children's Books, a division of Penguin Random House LLC, 1745 Broadway, New York, NY 10019, and in Canada by Penguin Random House Canada Limited, Toronto, in conjunction with Disney Enterprises, Inc. Random House and the colophon are registered trademarks of Penguin Random House LLC.

randomhousekids.com
ISBN 978-0-7364-3821-6 (trade) — ISBN 978-0-7364-8257-8 (lib. bdg.)
Printed in the United States of America
10 9 8 7 6 5 4 3 2 1

Chapter 1

"So where'd he come from?"

I can't tell you how often I get that question. Everyone is curious and a little bit baffled. So I'm here to set the record straight.

I'm Ray Reverham, the hard-driving crew chief for racing's surprise sensation, Jackson Storm. He's the out-of-nowhere superstar that everybody has been talking about since his big win at Copper Canyon Speedway.

I come from a long line of crew chiefs. I guess you could say racing is the family business. I've seen a lot of crazy things in my years of running racing teams, but I've never experienced anything quite like the Jackson Storm story.

The rumors I hear about Storm always give me a good laugh. I've been asked if Jackson Storm was made in a laboratory from spare parts by a mad scientist. I've also heard the theory that he's controlled remotely by a supercomputer with artificial intelligence. There's even a rumor that his engine came from an alien spaceship that crash-landed in the desert.

Let me start by saying that while they're exciting, these theories are nonsense. Jackson Storm is simply a very fast, very talented race car with an unlikely background.

So what's his deal, then? How does someone just cruise onto the racing scene like that, without anyone seeing him coming? It's really no mystery. It's just that Jackson Storm didn't take the usual path to Piston Cup stardom.

It all started when I received an invitation from Axle P. Biggs, a business tycoon. I had no idea what I was in for when I arrived at his headquarters high atop Biggs Tower.

"Welcome, Ray!" Biggs boomed. "May I call you Chief?"

"Sure, everybody does," I replied, following him into his spacious office.

"I'm a man of action, not words, Chief, so let me cut right to the chase: I'm preparing to shock the racing world. And I want to know if you're interested in coming along for the ride."

"Okay," I said, distracted by the panoramic view of Los Angeles from his windows.

"Beautiful, isn't it?" Biggs said. "When you're

this high up, the sky's the limit. That's exactly what I was thinking when I made plans to build the most advanced racing facility in the world."

"I didn't know Biggs Industries was involved with racing," I said.

"Well, I wasn't. Not until my son A. P. Biggs Jr. showed interest in the sport," Biggs replied. "He gave me the idea to win a Piston Cup."

I smiled. "You can't just build a pricey facility and expect to win a Piston Cup," I told him.

"Well, you haven't seen this racing facility yet," Biggs said. He rolled over to a table to show me a model of the proposed facility. I could tell he was proud of it. "The Biggs Industries Racing Complex will feature the most technologically advanced training equipment. And you, Chief, will help me find and train racing's next superstar."

"The process is a little more complicated than that," I replied.

"Listen, Chief," he said, rolling behind his massive desk. "I'm an entrepreneur. I started my business empire with computer software, then created an Internet search engine, and, most recently, got into security systems—all areas I had no experience in. I know how to identify opportunities and hire the experts and talent to help me achieve my objectives. Why should racing be any different?"

"There are just a lot of factors involved in winning a Piston Cup," I told him.

"You leave those factors to me," he said. "Your job is to focus on finding the next big thing for Team Biggs. I know you're looking for a new opportunity. You were the crew chief for a legendary Piston Cup champion. You know what's required to get to the top. I think you should come aboard and give this a shot."

It was true. I *was* looking for an opportunity, as my last racer had recently retired. I was between race cars, as they say. I was nervous about working for someone outside the racing business, but Biggs was right: I needed the job, and the challenge was certainly unique.

"It sounds interesting," I said.

"That's what I thought you'd say!" Biggs exclaimed. "Now go find me my champion."

I couldn't help laughing out loud. "That's much easier said than done. Searching for the next big racing star isn't like—"

"Chief, I have no doubt that you're up to the task," he said, cutting me off. "Just remember, we have to move quickly. They don't call me Speedy Biggs for nothing!"

So I headed out to the heart of Piston Cup country to recruit ten racers. I called every connection I had. I traveled far and wide, went to more than a hundred junior-league races, and visited as many racing academies. I chased down rumors about street racers. I chatted up reporters for tips on up-and-coming speedsters and scouted every place I could think of for rookie talent I could mold.

I managed to round up nine young racers in the nick of time. The Biggs Industries Racing Complex opened three weeks ahead of schedule—and it really was the most technically advanced training facility I had ever seen.

The racers immediately began training on the simulators and treadmills. While they showed a lot of promise, they were an inexperienced lot.

They were also spoiled, and it was difficult to push them to their limits. There was only one racer, Tim Treadless, who seemed fast enough to qualify for a Piston Cup race, but I knew it would take a lot of work. Not one of them was the instant, out-of-the-box star Biggs wanted.

"I expected more from you, Chief," he said. "I gave you the facility, and you rounded up the best you could find, but there's nobody here who has star potential. My data expert is reviewing each racer's performance on the simulator, and he is concerned."

He had good reason to be. But so far, all we had were results from the racing simulator, which didn't give us a complete picture of the racers' capabilities and talent. We still needed to see them on a real track. In my opinion, no high-tech training could take the place of dirt and asphalt.

I sighed. "Give me a little more time with them," I said.

"I don't want to drag this out," said Biggs. "We have room for one more racer on this team. Find me a winner by the end of the week, or I'll find someone who can."

I don't want to say I was desperate, but I needed a miracle. And you won't believe where I found one.

Chapter 2

That night, I drove around the city thinking about the challenge Mr. Biggs had presented. It seemed that the odds were stacked against me— I was looking for buried treasure without a map.

That's when I happened to drive past a place that caught my eye. Packed with young cars, it was some kind of high-tech arcade, with loud music and flashing neon lights. There were about thirty cars lined up outside waiting to get in. I told the security guard by the door that I just wanted to take a look around, so he let me through.

There were rows upon rows of game stations in one gigantic room. All the players were completely immersed in virtual races. Some were playing against computer-controlled opponents, and others were taking part in tournaments with other gamers. Scores and rankings were constantly being updated on large monitors throughout the arcade.

Between the sounds of revving engines and all the chatter and music, it was difficult to hear anything. The place was buzzing . . . literally.

I knew I had to tell Mr. Biggs about this. So right there in the middle of all the noise, I called him.

"Mr. Biggs, maybe you should think about investing in one of these new racing arcades," I said. "I'm in one now, and the place is packed. You could probably make some money opening a chain of these."

Biggs was interested. "Hmmm," he said. "What's the main attraction?"

"A racing game called *SC3*—short for *Super Corsa 3*," I told him. "Apparently it's the latest craze. You should see how many cars are waiting to play it."

"Got it," Biggs said. "Chief, why don't you drop

by my office in three days and we'll have a chat."

I was pretty sure he was going to fire me. I was supposed to be finding racing's great new superstar, and here I was, hanging out in an arcade.

I showed up at his office three days later expecting the worst.

"Chief," said Biggs, "I'm glad you called me the other night. Since we last spoke, I bought the company that makes the *SC3* game."

"You did?" I asked, surprised. "Why?"

"You gave me an idea," he said. "That company had no vision. They made a good game, but they couldn't tap into its true potential. I have the tools to leverage that asset."

"Wait—what potential? What tools? What asset?" I was baffled.

He chuckled. "That company was focused on the storefront arcade angle. It's small-time stuff, and there's no way to scale that up. The real action these days is online. So I'm going to host a global online racing competition with SC3. We'll have the best players from around the world vying against each other. It'll be the biggest online racing tournament in history! My people are already working on it."

"And how does that help us?" I asked.

Mr. Biggs smiled. "I have some racing data on the cars who play SC3. Some of them have better times on the game than your nine racers do on our simulator. So I've decided that the winner of the online tournament will be crowned the best SC3 racer in the world—and will get the final open slot on my racing team."

"Whoa, whoa!" I said. "There's a big difference between winning an online game and winning a real race against professional race cars."

"There is?" Biggs asked. He seemed to be amused by my concern. "I think you're wrong on that score, Chief."

"Sir, have you even been to a—"

"C'mon," Biggs said. "A car, whether he races in a game or on a speedway, needs a foundation of essential skills—speed, instinct, great reflexes, and coordination, to name a few."

"I think you're dismissing the unique qualities required to compete in the Piston Cup," I replied.

"Oh?" Biggs said. "Really? And do you believe racers possess some kind of magical powers the rest of us can only imagine?"

There was something about his attitude that was annoying me. "It's not any kind of hocus-pocus, but racers like Lightning McQueen, Cal Weathers, and Bobby Swift do have special qualities that separate them from everyone else."

"Okay, Chief. Take me for an example," Biggs said. "In business school, nobody thought I'd have the success I've enjoyed. I wasn't special. I just worked harder, faster, and smarter than my classmates. And look at me now! I've left everyone in the dust."

I wasn't sure how to respond to that.

Biggs sighed. "You've got to trust me on this

one. What happens in the game will translate to the racetrack. Mark my words!"

"Mr. Biggs," I said, "that's like saying if you can watch a movie, you can be a movie star."

"To be frank, Chief, you don't have a better suggestion, so why don't you let me do what I do best. I build empires with bold thinking and superior ideas."

It seemed absolutely loony to me. But he was right. I couldn't propose an alternative plan. And at that point, I was ready to try just about anything.

Chapter 3

The first-ever *SC3* Global Online Racing Competition was held two weeks later. Biggs's office had been transformed into a command center for tracking his tournament. Monitors had been set up everywhere. Wires and cables crisscrossed the floor. Workers were watching the screens closely and calling out updates to each other.

"We have eighteen thousand contestants from all over the globe," Biggs said. "How's that for a fast turnaround? Our social channels are blowing up."

"I'm not even sure what that means," I mumbled.

Biggs introduced me to the car who crunched all his numbers. Biggs called him his data wrangler. I never got his real name, only his nickname: Stats.

"Stats, why don't you tell Chief how it's all going to work."

"This is a single-elimination bracket system that randomly pairs racers," Stats said, scanning the bank of computers in front of him. "Within an hour, we'll be down to nine thousand racers. An hour after that, four thousand five hundred will remain. By tonight, we'll have a winner."

"Now, that's what I call speed," Biggs chuckled.

"How do the races work?" I asked Stats.

The data expert looked excited to have someone interested in his project.

"Each online race takes place at a replica of a well-known, randomly chosen speedway," Stats explained. "Every detail is matched, from the apron to the infield to the ads on the walls. Two racers square off in a field of twenty other cars driven by the computer. Whoever can navigate a hundred and fifty laps without crashing, running out of gas, or getting beaten by the other racer moves on to the next round."

"That's impressive," I said.

"Excuse me, sir," Stats said. He turned to the crowd. "All right, everyone, I've got green flags ready across the board. The nine thousand initial races will begin in ten seconds and counting."

A hush fell over the room as everyone began to watch the monitors. There were so many screens and blinking lights, I didn't know where to look.

Stats called out the final countdown: "We are under way in five, four, three, two, one. GO!"

And off they went, virtual race cars battling it out on virtual racetracks.

It was the oddest experience for me. The *SC3* arcade had been noisy with computerized racing sounds, but here the volume was turned off. Only the hum of computers filled the air. It wasn't like the racing I enjoyed. I watched a few of the races, but they just didn't hold my interest.

The tournament continued through the afternoon. The losers were eliminated, and the winners were matched up against other winners. I had to give Biggs credit—everything was going exactly as he had planned.

I'm not going to lie, though. At some point, I dozed off. I must've been asleep for a few hours before the noise and excitement in Biggs's office woke me. I went in to see what was happening.

Everyone was gathered around a single screen, watching the two final racers battle it out. When the winner crossed the finish line, beating his opponent by two car lengths, the place exploded with cheers and hoots.

"We have our winner!" Biggs hollered, as if he'd just struck gold.

"So what happens now?" I asked.

SC3

1st JACKSON STORM

2nd HARVEY RODCAP

"This talented young racer gets his prize money," Biggs said, "which is electronically transferred right into his bank account. There's no delay when you work with Axle P. Biggs."

I looked at the screen. I couldn't figure out who had won. "Who's the lucky racer?"

Stats answered for Biggs. "His screen name is Jackson Storm, and believe it or not, he's right here in Los Angeles."

"You hear that, Chief?" Biggs said. "The kid is a local. He's right in our backyard! What are the chances of that?"

"Pretty slim," I said. "I've never heard of a great Piston Cup racer coming from L.A." I thought for a moment about the name Jackson Storm. It sounded familiar to me. "Wait a second. I think I saw that name on a screen at the arcade I visited the other night."

"See, things are already going our way!" Biggs exclaimed. He grinned at Stats. "We cast our net and caught our star racer. He was right under our grilles the whole time!"

"Indeed we did," Stats said, looking as if he'd

pulled off the feat of the century.

"So what do we know about this Jackson Storm?" I asked Stats.

"It's funny you mention that," Stats said, flashing through multiple screens on his computer. "I've been trying to figure that out, but he keeps a very low profile. It's like he's in stealth mode or something."

"A car with a mysterious background?" Biggs said. "We can work with that."

Stats made a grunting noise. "So strange. He has almost no presence on social media. He's a bit of a ghost. His name is mentioned a lot on message boards and online posts focused on *SC3*, but he never leaves any comments himself."

"The strong and silent type," Biggs said quietly. "That means we can build his backstory and his brand from the ground up. It's perfect."

"So where do I find this phantom car?" I asked Stats.

"He didn't put an address on his entry form," Stats said. "But he seems to be logged on right now at that arcade you visited the other night."

Biggs turned to me. "Okay, then, Chief—why are you idling? Head over there and track this kid down. Let's have some proper introductions. Then we'll start turning the wheels of commerce."

"Sounds like a plan," I said.

Biggs gave me his billion-dollar smile. "It's like I always say, Chief: When you move fast, good things happen. Now go get my champion!"

Chapter 4

On my second visit to the racing arcade, the place was even noisier, more crowded, and more chaotic than before. The air was electric with a celebratory mood: one of their own had just been named *SC3* champion of the world.

"I'm looking for the gamer with the screen name Jackson Storm," I said to a small forklift who had approached me.

"Who *isn't* looking for him?" the forklift said.

"I'm sure his popularity is soaring," I said, scanning the crowd.

The forklift rolled closer so I could hear him better in the clamor. "He just won a huge online racing contest and got a big prize. He's the best in the world tonight, so his profile is sky-high, if you know what I mean."

"I think I do," I said.

"Are you some kind of long-lost relative?" he asked.

"No," I replied.

"Do you need to borrow some money?"

"No."

"Do you want to challenge him to a race?"

"No."

"Is he in some kind of trouble?"

"No, nothing like that."

"Were you and him involved in a hit-and-run? It's illegal to leave the scene of an accident, you know."

I tried to keep my frustration in check. "Hey, c'mon, you seem like a nice forklift, but I don't really have time to play twenty questions."

Two cars, one blue and one red, rolled up to join our conversation.

"What do you want with Storm?" the blue one asked. "Are you an undercover cop?"

"Are you from the government?" the red one squeaked in a high-pitched voice. He had a lot of energy. Everything he said was followed by a nervous giggle. "Are you here to collect taxes from the big winner?"

I continued to look around as I talked to the cars, hoping I'd recognize Jackson Storm from the profile picture I'd seen back at Biggs's office.

He was a sleek, dark gray car with a confident smirk, but that's about all I could remember.

"Fellas," I said, "I'm not a cop, I'm not from the government, and Storm and I weren't involved in an accident. I want to talk to your friend about joining a race team."

"Well, he's not exactly a friend," the forklift said, backing up slightly. "I didn't say I was his friend. He doesn't roll that way. Let's just say we're acquaintances. And we're a little suspicious of strangers."

"We watch his back," said the red car with another nervous chuckle. "He's kind of big deal around here."

"Yeah, and online, he's a living legend," said the blue one.

"Well, yes," I said, "I do know that he won the *SC3* tournament tonight because I work for the company that owns the game. I have a matter to discuss with him."

Now they smiled at me.

"So this is like Storm's big break!" the forklift shouted.

"Wow, this is incredibly awesome!" the red car exclaimed.

"Uh . . . can we keep it quiet?" I said. "I want to respect Jackson Storm's privacy. Why don't you take me to him. I'm sure he'll be grateful."

They exchanged uncertain glances.

"Okay," said the blue car. "Follow us."

I followed them through the crowd, and they took me to a back corner. They pointed to where Jackson Storm was playing a game of *SC3*.

I was surprised. This kid had just played the game all day long, finished first in a high-pressure international competition, and won a nice chunk of change, and he was *still* playing.

I joined a group of cars who were watching him. They were all marveling at his expertise.

Storm racked up bonus points and fuel tokens with robotic precision. There was no hesitation in the way he played. He powered past the other cars in the game with an aggressive efficiency that revealed a high level of confidence, focus, and concentration.

He seemed disappointed when he finally reached the finish line and a checkered flag flashed across the screen. The flag was replaced by a rotating golden trophy that read SC3 CHAMPION. It had obviously been designed to look like the Piston Cup trophy. The small gathering cheered and whooped as Storm's name was inscribed on the trophy with a purple laser beam.

The moment Storm left the game console, the forklift was at his side in a flash, whispering to him. Storm met my eyes with a sharp glance of suspicion. After a few moments, he slowly rolled over.

"Can I help you, mister?" he said.

"Chief. You can call me Chief," I said.

"Okay ... Gus," he said, sizing me up. "You look like a Gus to me."

"Gus, huh? Well, call me whatever you like. I'm here representing Biggs Industries," I said. "I work for Mr. Biggs."

"And?" he said with an impatient sigh.

"Biggs acquired the company that made *SC3*, and we hosted the online racing competition today—which you just won."

"Yeah . . . I remember," he said, his eyes half closed.

"Uh, congratulations, by the way."

"Thanks, Gus," he said, clearly bored. "I've won lots of racing competitions."

"Okay, well, I swung by because we'd like you to come and meet with Mr. Biggs. He might have—"

"No thanks," he said, cutting me off.

This kid was working my nerves already, and I'd only been talking to him for less than a minute. He was cocky, unfriendly, and as cool as black ice. He seemed weary of the world, like he'd already lived a thousand years and nothing impressed him.

I noticed that the two protective cars and forklift were watching us with great interest. I moved in a little closer so Storm's lackeys couldn't hear.

"Let me cut to the chase," I said, "because I think neither of us likes to waste time. Mr. Biggs wants you to join his new racing team. He's built a high-tech training facility, and I'm in charge of getting his prospective racers ready for the Piston Cup series. He thinks you might have what it takes to be a real racing champion."

Storm sniffed and looked around the arcade before speaking.

"Well," he said, "thanks for the interest, Gus, but I like my independence. I can't see why I'd want a regular job with people bossing me around. Plus, my win today gives me some nice driving-around money."

I waited a moment. "Listen, this training facility has real racing simulators. If you think *SC3* is fun, you should drive on one of those. And Mr. Biggs sees great potential in you."

"Potential?" Storm said. "Everyone online is already tweeting, posting, and chatting about me. My name is *legend*."

"Okay, but that's in the virtual world. I'm talking about actual racing."

"I'm not sure, Gus," he said.

I finally lost my patience. "Cut me some slack and come meet Mr. Biggs. Besides, you're contractually required to meet with him—or you have to give back your winnings."

He rolled his eyes. "Okay, okay, take me to your leader. Let's get this over with."

It was a huge relief. I could almost imagine Biggs impatiently driving in little circles around his office, grumbling about how long I was taking to deliver his champion.

Chapter 5

When Storm rolled off the elevators on the hundredth floor at Biggs's headquarters, I could tell he had finally seen something that impressed him.

His eyes opened wide as he took in the polished marble floors, fancy wood paneling, and floor-to-ceiling windows with stunning views of the city.

"This place rocks," Storm said. "Now, *this* is my style."

I found it interesting that he would be so dazzled by a little shine and flash, which made me realize it was going to take me a while to figure him out.

"Welcome! Welcome!" roared Biggs, coming out of his office. "Wow, look at you. The living legend Jackson Storm! My *SC3* champion. Son, you look so fast, you'd probably get a speeding ticket parked at the curb."

"Uh, thank you?" Storm said, following Biggs into his stately office.

I was stunned myself when I rolled in. All evidence of the race had been swept away. No wires. No monitors. No Stats or the other workers.

Instead there was a velvet curtain that blocked off half the room. Biggs went over to a golden pedal near the curtain. He seemed to enjoy seeing the puzzled look on Storm's face.

Biggs cleared his throat. "Jackson Storm, I'm sure you think you've had a pretty good day. And I'm here to tell you that it's about to get even better. In fact, this is about to become the best day of your life."

Then Biggs rolled onto the golden pedal, and the curtain slowly opened. Behind it were framed posters, photos, and *SC3* advertisements—all featuring Jackson Storm's image. A large computer screen played a short animated clip of Storm winning the *SC3* trophy, a moment that was accompanied by the cheers of fans and a shower of gold and silver confetti.

How did he pull this off? I thought. Storm had won just a few hours ago. I had to give Speedy Biggs credit—he knew what he was doing.

It all had the desired effect on Storm. His eyes swept over his picture on the posters and ads, and he couldn't hide his smile. It was clear that nothing like this had ever happened to him.

"Whoa, dudes," Storm said. "This is mind-blowing."

That brought a roar of laughter from Biggs, and he gave me a secret wink. He was working his magic.

"Listen, Mr. Jackson Storm. You are at a crossroads," Biggs said in a silky voice I hadn't heard before. "This is one of those times in your life that you'll always remember. A fork in the road, if you will. I want you on my racing team, as I'm sure Chief has already told you. Now, I can't force you. You can do what you want. If you'd prefer, you can go back to being a big shot down at the arcade."

"Or?" Storm said when Biggs didn't continue.

"Or you can maximize the opportunity of a lifetime. I can see you becoming the icon, the symbol, the spokescar for my *SC3* franchise."

"That would be awesome," Storm said.

"It would be awesome for the game, for you, and for me," replied Biggs.

"Totally," Storm said.

"However, there's more beyond *SC3*," Biggs said. "Much more."

"More?" Storm asked, chomping down on the shrewd tycoon's hook.

Biggs positioned himself in front of the most impressive Jackson Storm poster in the room. "I need a star racer for my new team, and you could be it. If you're half as good on a real track as you are on *SC3*, you'll be winning in no time."

"Sounds like a no-brainer," said Storm.

"The deal is simple," said Biggs. "You'll train with Chief, qualify for the Piston Cup series, and win me a championship. But it's all or nothing. If you walk away, the *SC3* deal is history, too. No hard feelings—I'll just choose someone else. But if my hunch is right, you won't turn this down. It's a win-win for both of us. You become a household name, and I have a representative for my racing brand. There's just one condition: you have to do this my way."

Storm had stars in his eyes, but I could see him hesitating, his gears turning as he worked out what he'd have to give up if he said yes. No more independence. No more hanging out at the arcade. No more doing whatever he wanted. He knew that becoming a pro racer would take considerable commitment and sacrifice on his part. It was a big decision.

Biggs shot me a confident glance as we waited for Storm's answer.

"I'll need my own room," Storm said. "I don't like sharing a room. I'm private that way."

"Not a problem," said Biggs. "Everyone at the facility has their own room."

"You're not going to paint me, are you?" Storm asked. "If I'm going to be seafoam green or hot pink or something, I just can't do it."

Biggs looked at me, not sure what to say. "We have no plans to change your paint job . . . do we, Chief?"

"No plans at this time," I replied. "But you'll eventually get decals, and if everything works out the way we hope, you'll be assigned a number.

All that is pretty standard, but let's not get ahead of ourselves."

Lost in thought, Storm rolled slowly past the posters and advertising designs again, squinting at each one.

Now Biggs appeared a bit nervous. It was an expression I had not seen on him before.

I looked over at Storm again, trying to figure out what he was thinking. He was hard to read.

And just like that, the decision was made.

"Okay, let's do it!" Storm burst out.

Biggs looked so relieved and happy, he was glowing.

I cleared my throat. "Well, then—you better get some sleep."

"Sleep? No way! I'm gonna go celebrate!" Storm said.

Biggs leaned in. "I think what Chief is saying is that you've got a lot of work to do. And he likes to start early."

A look of fear and uncertainty swept across Storm's face, but only for a second. After a beat, his cocky smirk was back.

"Sure, whatever you say," he said. "You're the big boss, Gus. Aye, aye, Captain, and all that jazz."

The three of us shared an uneasy laugh.

I looked up at one of the posters of Storm and thought, *We'll know soon enough if his skills in the virtual world translate to the real world.*

Attempting to turn a gamer into a racer was either going to be the biggest mistake of my life or my greatest triumph. And honestly, it turned out to be a little of both.

Chapter 6

After the first few days of training, it became clear that Storm was a fierce competitor. Not that he didn't have a lot to learn. He certainly did, but the things that made him nearly unbeatable in *SC3* made him a force to be reckoned with among his new teammates.

Storm's transition to the high-tech racing simulators was almost seamless. He excelled from the moment he rolled onto one of the big, sophisticated machines. He found the precise features of the simulators thrilling, especially after mastering *SC3*'s more basic controls. In just hours, he was outracing his teammates, who had been training on the simulators for weeks.

"If anybody wants lessons on how to increase their scores on this simulator, I'm the car to see," Storm said to the other racers. "I'm happy to give you tips and pointers in exchange for some of your simulator time, since Gus is limiting me to just three hours a day. So come to the master if you're interested."

This did nothing to boost his popularity.

"Storm, I'd like to introduce you to our team captain and best racer, Tim Treadless," I said shortly after Storm's arrival.

"Welcome," Treadless said.

"Huh, I wouldn't have guessed you were at the

top of this team," Storm said, looking at Treadless like he was a broken piece of machinery.

"If you need anything, just let Tim know," I told Storm.

"Oh, okay, I'll do that," replied Storm. "And, Treadless, if you need lessons, don't hesitate to ask me. I've seen you on the simulator, and you could use some pointers."

"What did you say?" Treadless exclaimed.

I rolled between the two cars. "Easy, fellas— we're all in this together."

"Listen, Gus, I'm not here to make friends," Storm said.

"Mission accomplished," Treadless replied.

"The whole team concept is just not my thing," Storm continued. "I prefer to work—and race—alone."

"What a nice addition to the *team*, Chief," Treadless said.

"Cool it," I said to Storm.

"I'm as cool as ice," Storm said as he rolled

off. "Don't be so sensitive, Treadless. I was just joking."

"He's a gamer, not a racer," Treadless said after Storm had left.

"He's complicated," I said. "Give him time to adjust. He's a bit of a loner."

"I can see why," replied Treadless, rolling his eyes. He drove away without saying another word.

Storm fit in like a fifth wheel with the other racers as well. It certainly didn't help that he was the last one to join. The others were already used to each other. But Storm considered his teammates to be inferior and underqualified. In turn, they saw him as bossy and arrogant. Even worse, they figured he was part of a publicity stunt to boost subscription sales for Biggs's new *SC3* online racing community, not an actual candidate to represent the team on the track.

I pulled Storm aside one day on the way to the facility's wind tunnel.

"You've got to work harder at getting along, Storm," I said. "This isn't all about you winning.

It's about being the best you can be. A better race car. A better teammate. A better leader."

"Listen, Gus—I'll try harder to be the best Storm I can be," he said. "I won't get in anyone's way, as long as you stop with all the rah-rah, let's-all-be-one-happy-family stuff. Save that for the other cars."

The kid was a piece of work.

I decided to put him through his paces.

When he was late to team meetings, which was often the case, I gave him menial tasks, like answering the phones and mopping the hallways. If he failed to comply, I restricted his access to the simulator. But none of it fazed him. He was determined to stand up to whatever punishment I could dish out. He had an unwavering perseverance that I had to admire.

One night, I was reviewing the team's performance data in my office when I heard Storm hooting and howling in the simulator room. I was surprised to find him playing *SC3* on one of the simulators. Tim Treadless had mentioned that Storm was still playing his video game, but this was the first time I'd caught him in the act. I shut the power off.

Blinking in the sudden darkness, Storm said, "Oh, c'mon, Gus. I'm just blowing off some steam."

"How did you get *SC3* to play on the simulator?" I asked.

"Stats rigged this up for me. Pretty cool, huh?"

I sighed. "Time to get some sleep, Storm, so you're not late for another morning meeting."

After he left, I called Biggs, who liked an update at the end of each day.

"I don't know, Mr. Biggs," I said. "Storm's scores are off the charts, but he's hard to be around. He's not exactly making friends with the other guys."

Biggs sighed. "I've heard. But I'm looking to win, and win fast. As long as his behavior isn't a major distraction, we'll have to grin and bear it."

"Understood," I said. "The kid has incredible natural ability, but he's not used to discipline, structure, or teamwork. How do you take a cocky, hard-to-control brat and turn him into a racing champ?"

Biggs laughed. "Well, that's what I'm paying you to figure out."

"Mr. Biggs, I've been in this game a long time. I've been around champions before, and there's more to winning than just natural ability."

"I understand," Biggs said. "He just needs some guidance and mentoring to—"

"No, it's more than that," I said, cutting him off, not sure where I was going with this conversation. "It's . . . it's about character."

Biggs sighed. "Does he work hard?"

"Yes, he does. Very hard."

"Is he tough? Does he stick to it?"

"I'm not sure if it's toughness or stubbornness, but whatever it is, he's got plenty."

"Does he love to race?"

"He loves to race on the simulator, that much is clear."

"How about winning?"

"Yes, sir, he loves to win more than he loves racing, but that doesn't make him a winner."

"There's a difference, Chief?"

"Yes, I believe there's a difference between

winning and being a winner. I really do."

Biggs was silent for a few moments. "Well, Chief, I'm not sure what to say, except turn him into a winner."

"I understand, sir."

"Jackson Storm is a needle in the haystack," he said. "We struck gold with this kid. He's our diamond in the rough, and I'm counting on you to take that diamond and make it shine. Don't mess this up by overthinking things, Chief."

Before I could respond, the phone went dead.

"Yes, sir," I said.

I remained in my dim office, listening to the silence. I knew I had a lot of work ahead of me.

Chapter 7

While it was evident that Storm was in a class of his own on the simulator, word spread through the team that he had never actually been on a real racetrack.

That was a problem.

A racing game like *SC3*, while challenging and requiring a lot of skill, did not have the unpredictable conditions and distractions that affect racers in a competitive environment. With *real* racing comes *real* danger. Every racetrack is challenging in its own, unique way. You have to master the straightaways, corners, and banks, while paying close attention to the crosswinds, racing surfaces, weight distribution, grip, and downforce. And on top of all of that, you've got to maneuver around cars who are racing more than two hundred miles per hour just inches away from you. Real racing requires an incredible amount of focus and precision. If you lose your concentration—even for a split second—you can find yourself in some serious trouble.

While all of Storm's teammates had grown up racing on tracks against other cars and only needed time on the simulator to fine-tune their skills, Storm was the exact opposite. He needed to start logging time on a track, and soon.

"I don't know why you're so worried," said Storm. "I'm awesome on the simulator, so I'll be awesome on the track. Simple."

"You say that now," I replied. "Just wait until your tires hit the speedway. You might be singing a different tune then."

I made some calls and secured an hour of practice time for him at the Los Angeles International Speedway.

When we arrived, Storm was impressed by the size of the stadium. "This place is pretty cool," he said when he emerged from the tunnel, his gaze sweeping over the empty grandstands, infield, and track. "Where is everybody?"

"I got you some private workout time so you can get the feel of things," I said.

We headed out to the track and began to take a slow lap. I wanted him to get comfortable.

"I saw that some of your friends from the

arcade visited you last night," I said as casually as I could.

"Are you spying on me?" he asked.

"I just happened to see them listed in the visitors' log," I told him.

"Yeah, they stopped by," Storm said.

"What did they want?" I asked.

"Nothing," Storm said. "They said everybody was asking where I was. They said I should blow off this race-team job and go back to the arcade."

"Hmmm," I said, trying to read his reaction. "What did you say to that?"

Storm studied the track in front of us as we continued going around.

"Not the answer they wanted," he said finally. "It's tempting, of course. I can't stand all these drills, lessons, and meetings. And I don't fit in on this team. But I don't quit."

"It'll come," I said. "There's an old saying that when the student is ready, the teacher will appear. Maybe that's the situation we've got here. You seem ready to grow and push yourself. And part of that growth is learning to work with others, you know? You have to go along to get along."

Storm grunted. "My teammates are okay. They could do a little less complaining about me."

"And you could be a little nicer to them."

"Maybe," Storm replied. "I'm just focused on the most important thing here: racing. I've never been beaten on *SC3*, so why should racing on the track be any different? I'm here for the big payday. The arcade doesn't have much to offer me anymore."

"That's the right attitude," I said. "Let's see what you can do on the big stage, okay?"

After a few laps at fifty miles an hour, then sixty, then seventy, Storm took it up to just past a hundred. He looked pretty confident.

"Okay, let's open it up!" I told him through my headset.

Storm's roar filled the empty stadium. His speed and confidence seemed to build with every lap. The ground beneath my tires hummed and vibrated whenever he rocketed past me.

I thought Biggs's plan might actually work. After several more laps, I clocked Storm at two hundred and three miles an hour.

"That's what I'm talking about!" I shouted as Storm zipped by me.

The next time he passed, however, he looked distracted, uncomfortable, and annoyed. He soon pulled to a halt in front of me.

"What happened?" I asked. "Why'd you stop? You were looking great out there. You reached two hundred and three miles per hour. Biggs is going to be thrilled."

"I don't know, Gus," he said. "I think I'm done. Let's go."

"What? We still have forty minutes!" I said. "Why would we go?" I paused for a moment. "Are you all right?"

"It just feels . . . weird," he said.

"What does that mean?" I asked.

I could see him struggling to find the words to express himself. I gave him time and waited.

"It's . . . I don't know—it just smells bad," he said.

"*Smells* bad?" I roared. "It's a racetrack, not a rose garden!"

"And . . . the track feels strange, like it's shifting under my tires. And the wind is going the wrong way. It's blowing from the side. And the sun reflecting off the press box up there, it's irritating. And there's a car mowing the infield grass. And you keep talking to me through the headset. It's just totally distracting."

"You're bothered by your crew chief talking to you?" I asked. "That's what crew chiefs *do* during a race! And there's barely a breeze out here. I'm surprised you can even feel it. And the track isn't shifting. You're just driving through some marbles—that's what we call the small bits of tire rubber. You'll get used to all this in time."

"I know! I know! These distractions are just really annoying. They're throwing me off my game. *SC3* is so much cleaner . . . and it doesn't have any weird smells."

I could tell he was kind of freaking out, and I had half expected it.

"Listen," I told him, "this is real racing. Nobody cares if you can win on a simulator, or how many points you score in an online tournament. This is where it all leads. You've just got to adjust."

He didn't look convinced. I was losing him. But I had an idea.

"Okay, we can leave soon," I said, "but first I need you to take some laps wearing this." I attached a digital camera to his roof. "These magnets will keep it from moving around, and the camera has a built-in stabilizer so its video doesn't shake too bad. All you need to do is drive."

"I look ridiculous!" he exclaimed.

"Well, nobody's here, so what does it matter?"

"How am I supposed to drive with this thing?"

"Just ignore it. Watch the track. Now give me ten or twelve of your best laps. Ready, set, GO!"

And he did.

It seemed that all his embarrassment and frustration came pouring out of him on those laps. I clocked his speed at two hundred and five miles per hour in the final three. Even with the camera on his roof creating more wind resistance, Storm had already improved his speed. I couldn't wait to tell Biggs.

When he finally came to a stop in front of me after his sprint, Storm said, "I'm done. Are there any car washes around here? I feel dirty."

"I have no idea, Storm," I said with a groan.

"They really need to vacuum this track," he said. "They mow the infield grass, but they don't clean the track?"

"The track is fine," I said.

"There are skid marks going every which way," he said. "When you're going fast, it's enough to make you dizzy, or put you in a trance."

I laughed. "You're complaining about skid marks? Seriously? It's a racetrack! Welcome to the real world."

He sighed. "Maybe I should get my air filter

changed," he said under his breath. "It's probably full of gunk now."

"Would you just stop?" I said, amused at all his worries. "It's not full of gunk. You're fine. This track is fine. The air is fine. You're just used to virtual racing, that's all. That's why we're out here today—to ease you into real racing. I know you can do it."

Storm was quiet for a few moments, thinking.

"Hey, can I keep this camera?"

"No," I said. "It's team property."

"What are you going to do with the recording?" he said.

"We're taking it to a computer expert," I said. "He'll know what to do."

Chapter 8

Stats was parked in front of the bank of computers in the video control room of the racing complex. Storm and I were standing with him, watching the screens with great interest.

The footage from the camera Storm had worn on his roof as he tore through those twelve laps for me back at the L.A. Speedway was on the large monitor in the center.

"As you can see," Stats said, "I've run this footage through our mainframe computer and combined it with detailed data about that track. I've downloaded weather conditions from the exact time Storm was out there, like temperature, wind, and humidity. I've put it all together and crunched the numbers, as they say."

"What's all that stuff all over the video?" Storm asked.

"That's how we've visualized the data for you," Stats said. "Those graphics tells us where things went wrong."

"Wrong?" said Storm. "Gus says I got up to two hundred and five on a few laps."

"You did," Stats replied. "But only temporarily.

By analyzing your racing performance, we can compare the path you took on the track with the optimum path for maximum efficiency and velocity. We can also identify your errors."

"Cool, right?" I said.

Storm looked at me, perplexed.

"For example," Stats continued, "see how you're sweeping high up near the wall coming out of that turn? That's too soon. You can see

that your angle leaving the turn is robbing you of over three point two percent of your initial velocity into the straightaway."

"Really?" Storm said, studying the video and its overlaid grids. "Is that what the dotted line is?"

"Indeed," Stats said. "That shows the path you should have taken. We call that the racing line. It's nothing personal. The computer doesn't know you or care about your feelings. It just tells you how to improve your speed and efficiency."

Storm grinned, not taking his eyes off the video. "Okay. I get it."

"There's more," Stats said. "Like based on this video, the computer says you're too high."

"High?" I asked.

"Yes, he's riding too high," Stats said to me. "That's the computer's opinion, at least. Storm needs to hug the track—ride lower, reduce air friction, minimize drag."

"We need more wind-tunnel work," I said, turning to Storm. "And you need to study these videos."

"I get it now," Storm said, still watching himself

rip around the track. "It's just like a video game, but it's out in the real world!"

Storm had seemed interested in what Stats had come up with, but when I switched out his simulator's usual digital interface with the video Stats had created, he blew a gasket. Storm had grown so accustomed to his virtual racetracks that the real-life L.A. Speedway footage covered with data, grids, dotted lines, and plotted paths was a shock to his system. It was nothing like the ultra-clean, high-resolution racetrack graphics of the simulator. I had taken away his favorite toy.

"Whoa! Whoa! Whoa!" he said, turning around. "What did you do? I want to race on the simulator. I've already seen that jittery video. I learned my lesson. I get it. I really do. But I want my simulator back . . . like, now!"

"You can't just watch the live footage once," I told him. "You need to live and breathe it."

"Okay, then at least let me warm up with *SC3*," he said. "I can earn twice as many points, extra lives, and pit-stop passes as any of the racers on our team, and in half the time. I can drive circles around the other guys!"

"Lower your voice," I said. "We've gone over this, Storm. Forget about that virtual stuff and focus on the real world. Just think of all the things you've got to get right to win a real race. When you're out there, it won't be a game anymore—it'll be a sport. Winning a real race is no joke. Trust me, I've seen my share of hotshots flame out once their tires hit the track."

Storm's eyelids drooped, which signaled to me that he'd stopped listening. "Lecture over?" he asked.

"If you had half the focus of Tim Treadless, you'd actually be dangerous," I said out of frustration.

"If he had half my talent and speed, I might care!" Storm shouted.

"Shhh," I warned. Other racers were down the hall, looking at us. "Okay, let's cool it. It's time to kick up our training a few notches, and we'll see how much you really want to win."

"More than you think," he said.

***

I spent hours in the wind tunnel working with Storm, trying to get him to stay lower to the ground at higher speeds to reduce air friction. The resistance slowed him down enough to make a sizable difference in his timing.

"It's only air!" he shouted from inside the wind tunnel. "It's not that big a deal!"

"Oh, yes it is," I said through the intercom. "You gotta stay low as you go. There's too much drag in your bag!"

"Please don't ever say that again," he said.

He spent so much time in that tunnel, he nearly fell asleep a few times.

After a week of intensive work, we were making real progress. But that was when things went off the rails.

We had the first safety incident in the short history of the Biggs Industries Racing Complex. And of course Storm was involved.

We had been working on pit stops—I had him practice pulling into the pits and then reentering the race. On one turn, Storm pulled out too aggressively and bumped Tim Treadless, clipping him hard enough that the whole exercise ground to a halt.

"News flash!" Treadless yelled at Storm. "This isn't a video game! I'm a real racer!"

As our safety crew tended to Treadless, I asked the other racers to give us some room.

"That was an accident," I told Treadless. "It wasn't intentional."

"Oh, you're going to take his side?" he snapped.

"I'm sure they can buff that out," Storm said. "Toughen up, Treadless. You'll be fine."

Treadless shot me a look of anger and resentment.

"You've got to be more careful, Storm!" I shouted.

"Hey, I guess I'm just used to merging with computer-controlled cars," Storm said. "They don't drive as hesitantly as ol' Timid Treadless here."

As Storm rolled off, Treadless and the other racers let him through. But they watched him pass in an awkward silence.

That was when I knew Storm was truly on his own.

Chapter 9

We lost four racers shortly after the collision between Storm and Treadless. They gave different reasons for leaving, but clearly Storm was creating an overly competitive and stressful environment. And the workouts were more intense than they could handle.

This actually worked in Biggs's favor, as he wanted to thin out the remaining lineup. He wanted me to focus on the few cars who could actually qualify for a Piston Cup. He was still determined as ever to have a race car represent Biggs Industries in this year's Piston Cup season.

"Good morning," I greeted my racers at the pre-training meeting I held every day. "As you know, there are six of you left, and I want to take this opportunity to say I appreciate all the hard work each of you is putting in. I understand that this training is extremely difficult. I know it's not for everyone. And I'm afraid it's—"

Just then, Storm rolled in, yawning. "Sorry," he said when he saw my glare.

"As I was saying, the training is about to become even more challenging, so I need all of you to stay strong and focused. You're going to have to work your hardest to prove to both Mr. Biggs and myself that you have what it takes to be a Piston Cup racer."

Twenty minutes later, I had all the racers get on treadmills. This wasn't our usual endurance exercise, though. I had set up an industrial fan to blow exhaust from a diesel generator right into their faces.

"WINNERS AREN'T BOTHERED BY BAD SMELLS AND EXHAUST!" I shouted above the roar of the fan.

Storm gave me a sideways glance. He knew I had designed the drill just for him. But his look of resentment was quickly replaced by one of steely determination. He coughed and grimaced but kept going on the treadmill.

Later, the cars raced in a tight, single-file formation around the complex's small racetrack. I had hung mirrors around each turn so that glaring reflections of light would flash in the racers' eyes. I could hear Storm grunt with each painful squint.

I'd also asked an old dump-truck buddy of

mine to sprinkle the track with a load of marbles, the tiny bits of tire. The horrified face Storm made as he drove over the marbles was priceless. Best of all, as the cars circled the track, I sang irritating songs and told bad jokes through the intercom system.

I had to hand it to Storm—he managed to continue the training despite all the distractions and obstacles. And he was outperforming all of his teammates.

I asked Stats to reprogram the wind tunnel to give us some extreme conditions. He later informed me that I could now push it up to hurricane-speed winds, which I immediately tried as a crosswind exercise. The cars hated it, of course. After twenty minutes of gale-force crosswinds, one racer quit on the spot. He sped, gasping, out of the wind tunnel, and I never saw him again.

Storm, however, only narrowed his eyes and gritted his teeth in the superpowered winds. He was determined to stand up to every challenge I gave him. He wanted to prove that he wasn't a quitter. And I wanted him to prove that he could handle whatever came at him in a real race. Storm was transforming into a professional racer right before my eyes.

The tough conditions also seemed to inspire Tim Treadless to dig deeper. He was focused solely on one-upping Storm. This led to a situation I couldn't have predicted.

One night during their free time, Storm and Treadless convinced Stats to wire two of the simulators together so they could race each other. This was against my simulator-room rules, but I'm sure they didn't tell Stats that.

Cheered on by his teammates, Treadless put pressure on Storm. No matter how quickly Storm accelerated, cut corners, or picked up pit-stop passes, he couldn't shake the racer from his tail. Storm's frustration grew.

Just as the final lap was ending, I entered the room to see what all the commotion was about. The cars on the screen were locked in a push down the straightaway. It was hard to tell who crossed the finish line first, but when the game flashed a photo-finish image, it was clear that Treadless had won by an inch or two.

As far as I knew, this was the first time anyone had gotten a better time than Storm on the simulator.

"YOU CHEATED!" Storm shouted as Treadless and the other cars celebrated the victory.

"WHAT IS GOING ON?" I thundered.

The room went silent and everyone froze.

But I had arrived too late.

Storm almost crashed into me as he raced out of the room.

He shot down the hallway, barreled into the complex's main entryway, and started doing doughnuts. His squealing tires left long black skid marks on the marble floor.

I couldn't believe what I was seeing.

He continued to whip around and around. The screeching of his tires was deafening, and the acrid air from the burning rubber soon stung my eyes. Storm became engulfed in the thick gray smoke that filled the room.

Stats's voice came at me from behind. "He'd better watch out or he'll set off the—"

Before Stats could finish his sentence, all the sprinklers in the facility popped to life and cold water rained down on everyone. Red lights flashed above the doors. An alarm blared in warning.

"Turn those sprinklers off," I told Stats, and headed out to confront Storm.

I found him parked sullenly in the middle of the big entryway, water showering down on him. "I CAN'T BELIEVE THIS! WHAT IN THE WORLD WERE YOU THINKING?" I yelled.

He looked up and blinked at me through the drops.

The sprinklers, flashing lights, and alarms stopped abruptly.

"Well, I feel a little better now," Storm said.

"Look at this mess!" I roared, pointing to the black ribbons of burned rubber circling the once-spotless floor. "Everything in this place is soaked!"

"Those smoke sensors are way too sensitive," he said.

"You're blaming the *sprinklers*?" I shouted. "Outside!" I followed Storm out the door. I didn't want to have it out with him in front of his teammates.

"You need to start showing some maturity!" I boomed at him once we'd left the building.

"Too late for that," Storm said, his eyes downcast.

"Why do you even want to race?" I asked.

"What?"

"Why do you even want to race?" I repeated.

"I don't know. Because I'm good at it, I guess. The first time I played *SC3*, I felt—"

"NO! Not the dang game! Why do you want to be a professional race car?" I persisted.

"Seems easy. Make some bank."

"Money? Money disappears as fast as it arrives," I said.

"Nothing like being recognized as I roll down the street."

"Fame? Forget fame. Fame is fleeting, too," I said. "I've seen a lot of racers come and go. And in time, your window of opportunity will also close. You have to make the most of this. You've got to be racing for the right reasons."

"I guess I just want to win a Piston Cup," he said. "Once I win, nobody can take that away from me. If I don't win, I'm just a participant."

"Sure, okay, but it's also about respecting the sport, your fellow teammates, the other racers, potential danger . . . and other people's property," I said. "You said it yourself: you need to be the best Jackson Storm you can be."

"I guess," Storm said, taking a deep breath. He glanced at the front door, lost in thought. "I was always bored and never good at anything, really, until I discovered *SC3*. That became my home. I was only happy when I was racing in a game. I'm just not great at hanging around other cars. You've seen me. I'm horrible at it—telling jokes, being pals, grabbing a pint of oil or whatever it is cars do together."

I rolled up close to him. "Listen, everyone has personal challenges to overcome, even me. My dad was lot tougher on me than I am on you. I was never good enough for him. Never worked hard enough. Once, after he watched me train some young racers for him, he pulled me aside and said I might want to think about pursuing another career. And I had grown up dreaming of being a crew chief, just like him. How do you think that felt? To be such a disappointment?"

"Pretty bad," Storm said. "But you showed him in the end, right?"

I exhaled. "I suppose. But hearing what he said lit a fire in me—a fire that still burns today. You need that kind of fire, that focus. You've got to show you can grow, and mature, and keep your eyes on the prize. You can't blow this opportunity with temper tantrums over losing a silly game."

He sighed. "Yeah, I guess I overreacted a bit. I need to go for a drive. I need some alone time."

"ALONE TIME?" I yelled, startling him. "You're not going anywhere! You're going to mop every square foot of that facility."

"What is it with you making me mop all the time?"

"It builds character," I said. "And you need all the character you can get."

"Not sure I agree with you on—"

"Oh," I said, interrupting him, "you're also going to apologize to every racer in that building, starting with Treadless."

"I'm not sure that's necessary," he mumbled.

"I don't really care what your thoughts are on the matter!" I snapped. "If you want to continue on this team, you will apologize, and you'll show some grace and humility when you do it."

"All right already! Sheesh," he said. "Don't get so worked up. You're going to snap a timing belt or something." Storm was silent for a few moments before making a small groaning noise. "Are you going to tell Mr. Biggs?"

"Are you kidding me? There's no chance he doesn't already know."

Chapter 10

Much to his chagrin, Storm's second trip to the Los Angeles International Speedway wasn't as private as the first one.

The grandstands were just as empty, but this time a class of about twenty-five young cars was gathered on the infield grass. Their voices echoed off the empty bowl of the speedway while an overwhelmed-looking teacher tried to shush them.

Storm's practice time on the speedway was going to be shared with a school field trip.

Storm froze the moment he saw the crowd of rambunctious cars. He was about to turn away when one of them called out to him.

"Hey, are you a real race car?" she asked.

"Rev your engine, dude!" another shouted.

"Are you rich? How much money do you make?" a pesky young car asked.

"Can you go faster than two hundred miles an hour?" asked another.

Storm looked at me. "I'm not sure I can do this."

"Because of some young racing fans?" I asked.

"I can't stand all the questions," Storm mumbled.

"Hey, do you know Lightning McQueen?" one of the students asked.

Storm looked at the young cars for the first time. "Never heard of him," he said.

"WHAT?" the same car shouted. "What kind of racer *are* you? Lightning McQueen is only the fastest, most awesome race car EVER!"

"Good for him," Storm grumbled.

"What about The King? Have you heard of him?" asked another young car.

"No."

"You really don't know much about the racing

world, do you?" I said with a sigh.

"You know what, Gus?" Storm said. "I'm not feeling it today. Let's bag it. I'm outta here." He surveyed the crowd of excited kids once more, then started to turn back toward the tunnel we'd entered through.

"Oh, no you don't," I said, blocking his way. Then, in a voice loud enough for all the young cars to hear, I roared, "Hey, Jackson Storm—why don't you show these curious young fans how you're going to win the Piston Cup!"

The cars exploded with whistles and squeals of delight. They were just twenty feet away, so it was hard not to be impressed by their youthful enthusiasm.

Storm, however, was *not* impressed. He sneered at me, unhappy to be backed into a corner. "I just told you I'm not feeling it today. The answer is no. I'm not racing."

I rolled up close to Storm. "Listen, I didn't want to say anything, but Mr. Biggs invited these cars here today to watch you practice. This is his son's class."

"Well, nobody asked me," Storm said. "Plus, they're rude and annoying."

He tried to drive around me again, but I continued to block his path.

"Knock it off. You can't bail every time you're uncomfortable." I said. "Mr. Biggs is up in the press box watching you right now. This was all his idea. And for your information, I usually don't have to beg a racer to race. They're normally happy to have the chance. So check your attitude at the curb."

Storm stared at me but finally closed his eyes. "Whatever. Let's get this over with."

I attached the camera to Storm's roof, as I'd done before, but this time it had been modified: a small antenna would send a live video feed to a large TV screen set up for the students. When the feed from the camera sprang to life on the screen, they gathered around to ooh and aah.

"Hey, I can see myself on the TV!" one girl screamed, and all the youngsters began to jump around and make silly faces for the camera.

Storm quickly turned away, and they disappeared from the screen.

"Okay, listen up, everybody," I announced to the young fans. "That car over there is Jackson Storm. He and I have been working very hard. He's a new racer, but I'm excited for his future. And I'm very proud of him. I have a feeling many of you will start hearing his name in the near future."

I could see Storm turning to look at me, but

I didn't take my eyes off the students.

I cleared my throat. "So . . . I'd like to give all of you the opportunity to watch him take some practice laps, and to see the track from his point of view—when the world flashes by him at more than two hundred miles an hour!"

The kids cheered.

I turned to Storm. "Okay, Storm, let's—"

Before I could finish, Storm revved his engine so suddenly and loudly that even I jumped back in surprise. The ground trembled under our tires. The young cars froze in absolute silence for a few seconds. Then Storm took off with a screeching, explosive start. The stadium filled with his husky rumble and jet-engine roar. I knew instantly that he was giving it his all.

The young fans immediately became caught up in the spectacle of seeing a race car whip past them. They were exhilarated to be so close to such power and speed.

"I've never seen a car move like him. He's amazing!" one car exclaimed.

"He works for my dad!" another shouted.

"That means he sort of works for me, too."

I glanced over and saw Axle P. Biggs Jr. looking very proud and confident. He was definitely a chip off the old block.

He saw me notice him and rolled over. "Hey, you're Chief, aren't you?"

"That's correct," I said, keeping my eyes on Storm.

"You know who I am?"

"Yes, I do," I said. "Nice to meet you. You must be excited to share this with your classmates."

He watched Storm rocket past us, then

continued. "My dad says you work hard but don't have the same sense of urgency that he does."

"Some things can't be rushed," I said. "And some things shared in private should probably be kept private, you know? Just a little bit of advice for you there, junior."

"Oh, sure," he said, embarrassed. "Good point. Anyway, Storm is awesome. Great job." He rolled off to join his hooting classmates.

The students cheered every time Storm zipped past. He had won them over with his sheer speed.

I timed Storm on his last twenty laps and was pleased to see he had broken his personal record. Again.

He didn't show any signs of tiring, so when our hour was nearly over, I picked up some headphones and told him it was time to wind down.

Storm rumbled through a dozen cooldown laps and met me near the tunnel.

"Well done," I told him. "That was great! New personal best."

"I tried to stay lower, like we've been practicing," he said. He seemed pleased with himself.

"Hey, racer guy," one fan called from the infield. "I bet you're almost as fast as Lightning McQueen!"

"Thanks," said Storm. Then he turned to me. "Whoever this Lightning is, I guarantee you he's not faster than me."

"Well, if you're going to win a Piston Cup, he's the one you'll have to beat."

"Students! Students!" the teacher called as

she shepherded her rowdy class over the track and toward the tunnel. "Let's all say thank you to Mr. Justin Storm."

"THANK YOU, MR. JUSTIN!" the class said in unison.

"It's *Jackson* Storm," the racer replied.

"Kids, you were a great audience," I said. "Who wants a Team Biggs racing decal?"

"I do! I do!" they all screamed.

When I looked back, Storm was already entering the tunnel. I'm sure he was glad for the chance to make a stealthy exit.

Chapter 11

The next day, Storm and I were summoned to Biggs's office for an unscheduled meeting.

Once we rolled off the elevator, we were asked to wait. We stared silently out one of the big windows in the reception area. After fifteen minutes, Storm became impatient.

"I thought he was calling us here to congratulate us on those top speeds yesterday," Storm said.

"That might be the case," I said.

"Then why is he making us wait so long?"

"Not sure. Maybe he got a phone call," I said.

"I don't have time for this!"

"Not so loud, Storm," I said, trying to calm him

down. "Mr. Biggs has a lot going on."

"Oh, and I've got nothing better to do?" Storm headed for the elevator. "I don't like this. I'm outta here."

"C'mon, just relax, would you? It's not like—"

I was interrupted by a loud click from the double doors that led to Biggs's office. The heavy doors swung open slowly and evenly, as if they were activated by remote control. Biggs didn't emerge to greet us as he usually did.

"Come in," he commanded from somewhere inside. Storm and I exchanged a look and entered. I led the way.

"Sorry to keep you waiting," Biggs said from behind his desk.

His office looked empty. There was no evidence of the posters and advertisements featuring Storm that had adorned the room on our previous visit. This time, it was all business.

Biggs cleared his throat. "I'm not one to mince words, so let me get right down to it. This has been a difficult decision, Storm, but we've decided to drop you from the team."

"WHAT?" Storm and I shouted at the same time.

"I wanted to tell you two together because—"

"Wait a second!" I said. "Why wasn't I consulted on this decision? This needs to be discussed!"

"The decision is final," Biggs said.

Storm had trouble finding words. "Why . . . why . . . why would you do something that makes NO sense? Did you see my times from yesterday? Have you even been listening to Gus? I'm the best racer you've got!"

"Take it easy," I said to Storm. "Let me handle this."

"Why should I?" Storm snapped at me. "He's firing *me*!"

"What's going on here, Mr. Biggs?" I asked as steadily as I could. "Storm is right. He is clearly the fastest racer on the team, and the one who is most likely to win you a Piston Cup."

Biggs sighed. "That may be the case. And yes, I have been reading your reports and reviewing the data with Stats on a daily basis. Storm has indeed improved considerably. But my concerns lie outside what the stopwatch can tell us."

That last part worried me. It would be hard for me to make a case for Storm if this wasn't about speed or racing.

"Look," I said, trying to think on my tires, "even Storm would agree with me that he's a little rough around the edges. Maybe he could work on his social skills, get some media training, but he's making incredible—"

"Stop right there, Chief," Biggs said. "I think you're blinded by your desire to get him in the winner's circle. A while ago, you told me there's a difference between winning and being a winner. I told you to make Storm a winner. Now I realize I asked you to do the impossible. Being a winner requires things like personality, charm, likability, and—"

"This isn't a popularity contest!" Storm yelled.

Biggs looked at Storm. "You and Tim Treadless have both been impressive. But—and this is nothing personal—we've decided to go with Tim as our spokescar. He's the whole package: Smart. Fast. Friendly. A great symbol of what we're trying to achieve here with the Biggs Racing brand."

"I can't believe this!" Storm shouted. "You're taking charm over performance? You're choosing a friendly smile over two hundred and five miles per hour?"

"Mr. Biggs, why is this decision being made now?" I asked. "What's the rush?"

"Buying that *SC3* game sped up my timetable," Biggs said. "This is a business decision. It's nothing personal. Racing data is important, but that's not the only kind of data. We've conducted focus groups. Tim's scores with the public are off the charts. His likability index is almost the best my marketing consultants have ever seen."

"*Likability index?*" Storm roared. "*Seriously? What's that got to do with racing?*"

I waved a tire at Storm to quiet him. "But Storm has a better chance of winning than Treadless does, guaranteed," I said. "You need to rethink this."

Mr. Biggs fixed his cool eyes on me for an uncomfortably long moment before speaking. "In case you haven't been paying attention, Chief, I didn't get to where I am today by *rethinking* my decisions. And if we must be frank here, Storm is unpredictable, reckless, and rude."

"He could use a little polish, sure, but—"

"I saw how he behaved at the track yesterday," Biggs growled. "The moment he saw those young fans, he tried to head for the exit. And I've heard all about the training accident with Tim Treadless. The way Storm handled that was embarrassing. Whatever happened to sportsmanship? Then there's the case of the expensive water damage from the fire sprinklers being set off—because Storm had a *temper tantrum*!" He looked down at the floor before continuing. "I didn't even need to ask who had the meltdown."

I couldn't think of anything to say. It was all true.

Biggs eyed Storm. "These incidents are evidence of poor character. I know your type, Storm. You'd never take second position behind Tim. And you haven't proven to me that you'd be a good teammate, which is why I am asking you to leave. Some flaws cannot be fixed."

"You know what?" Storm said, looking at me. "He doesn't really care about winning. He only cares about game sales and making money off someone else's hard work. I'm outta here!"

Storm left the office, rolled onto a waiting elevator, and was gone.

I was sure I'd never see him again.

"You'll have to make more progress with Tim Treadless now," Biggs said after a minute of awkward silence.

"No," I said.

"No what?" Biggs asked.

"No, I have to go, too," I said. "I should have been consulted on this decision before it was made. I'm just as much a part of this team as you are. Thank you for the opportunity, but I must resign from my position as your crew chief. I'll collect my things from the office today and say goodbye to the staff."

Without another word, I drove out of Biggs's office for good.

***

Later that day, I was still in shock as I rolled away from the complex for the last time. I was in a fog, lost in thought. It had all gone so bad so fast. I was outside the front gates when a voice I had thought I'd never hear again called out.

"Gus, we need to talk."

I turned and blinked twice. It was Storm.

"What are you doing here?" I asked. "I can't imagine why you'd want to talk to me."

"Well, there aren't many cars I *can* talk to," he said.

"Sorry about earlier," I said. "Biggs caught me off guard. I didn't see that one coming at all."

"Yeah, that caught me off guard, too," replied Storm. "I thought he was calling us in to praise us and give us the green light."

"Apparently not," I said. "Just the opposite."

"It's hard to know who to trust," said Storm, looking into the distance. "I trust you, though. You've always been fair to me. Firm, but fair."

"That's what I always aim to be," I said. "I had to quit, too. Can't have decisions like that made without my knowledge. I wasn't a great fit there anyway."

"That's why I'm here," Storm said.

"What do you mean?"

"After I left Biggs's building, a representative from another racing team was waiting for me across the street. He'd been tipped off."

"Really? Who tipped him off?" I asked.

"No idea," he said. "But it turns out his team wants me to race for them. It's IGNTR, which is a great sponsor. They have a nice facility. They know what they're doing."

"That's great, Storm!" I said. "They *are* a top-notch sponsor. And you've worked so hard. You really have improved in so many ways. You've earned the right to compete at the highest levels. I'm excited for you."

"But I told them I have one condition if they want me to sign with them," he said.

"What's that?"

"I said I'll only sign if they hire you as my crew chief," he said. "I know I have a lot to learn, but I think we work pretty well together."

I was silent for a moment, taking it all in. "Boy, this day has been filled with twists and turns, hasn't it?"

"Maybe I have trust issues," he said, "but with you on my side, I think my chances are better. *Our* chances are better."

"Well, look at us, landing on all four tires so quickly," I said with relief. "But listen, I have one condition, too: you have to change your attitude. No more bad sportsmanship. No more running away when things don't go your way."

"That's more than one condition," Storm said with a laugh. "But okay! Whatever you say. Let's go win a Piston Cup."

"I've seen what you can do," I said. "I don't want you to throw it all away because you can't control your temper or be gracious when it's called for. I believe in you, Jackson. You've got to start believing in yourself."

"I already said okay," he said. "Now let me introduce you to our new sponsor. They're waiting to meet you."

And just like that, one of my darkest moments was instantly transformed into one of my greatest.

Chapter 12

Storm had come a long way from being the game-obsessed hotshot I'd encountered so many months before in a crowded racing arcade. Now he was ready to do whatever was required to make it to the Piston Cup for our new sponsor, IGNTR.

As I expected, he not only qualified to compete for the Piston Cup, he did so well with IGNTR that he became the talk of the racing tabloids.

Half my time was spent turning down media requests for interviews. I needed to keep Storm focused on racing, not on explaining his unconventional background. Plus, I could never really predict what he'd say, so it was best to keep him a bit of a mystery at this early stage of his career.

He used to snicker at me when I lectured him and his teammates about forging your own destiny and creating your own luck. Now he was a true believer.

In the final hour before his first Piston Cup race, Storm was so amped up, I was surprised his tires were still on the ground. While we milled around during that dead time between practice laps and reporting for the start of the race, my job was to keep him from doing anything he'd regret and to bolster his confidence.

"This is amazing," he said, taking in the hustle and bustle of racers going through their final preparations with their racing teams.

"Remember, we stick to the plan we've discussed a million times," I told him. "I don't want you expending all your energy in the first fifty laps, then crossing the finish line at the back of the pack. If you work the plan, no one will be within twenty lengths of you at the finish."

"Got it," he said, but he wasn't really listening. His eyes were on the commotion around him.

"Hey, look," one race car said to another as they rolled past us. "Isn't that Online Jackson?"

"Sure looks like it," said the other. "What's he doing here?"

"Hey, Jackson!" said the first racer. "If you're looking for the arcade, it's that way!" That brought a hearty laugh from both cars.

"Jerks," Storm mumbled, watching them go.

"Don't worry about that stuff," I said. "They're just trying to rattle you."

Storm paused to look at a racer who was surrounded by the press. "That must be Lightning McQueen," he said.

I turned and saw the legendary Number 95 giving interviews and posing for photos. "Now, there's a racer who's earned the respect and admiration of the racing community across the globe," I said.

"He doesn't look like much," Storm said. "Well, he's never seen anything like me. I'll be on his radar soon enough. And he'll be behind me."

I sensed it was time to refocus Storm and give him a little pep talk.

"Listen," I said, "don't worry about Lightning McQueen. Never mind what these other racers say to you. Forget about the bad smells. You've worked hard to get to this moment, so don't get distracted. Show these guys why they should know the name Jackson Storm."

"Good luck," a voice suddenly called.

Storm and I turned and saw Stats rolling by.

"What are you doing here?" I asked.

"Oh, I'll be writing up some scouting reports for Mr. Biggs," he said. "I'm really glad it worked out for you two and my friends at IGNTR."

That was when it hit me. "So *you* were the one who told them about Storm, and that's how they knew when he was being let go."

Stats was too smart to answer. He gave us a sly wink. "Hey, I'm sorry about how it all went down," he said. "For what it's worth, you both should know I didn't agree with Mr. Biggs on his decision to cut Storm from the team. We don't always see eye to eye."

"Thanks, Stats, I appreciate that," Storm said.

"The data clearly pointed to you as our best shot, Storm," Stats said. "But Mr. Biggs has his own agenda. He told me some decisions were above my pay grade."

"No hard feelings," I said. "Thanks, Stats, for tipping off your friends at IGNTR."

"I can neither confirm nor deny that I said anything to them," he said, rolling off. "That'll be our little secret."

We watched him join the crowd making their way to the stands.

"ALL RACERS, FINAL CALL TO THE TRACK!" a voice blared over the loudspeaker.

"Okay, it's time to shock the world," I said to Storm. "I'll be on the headset, so just do your thing. Remember, I want you to hold back in this race."

"I know . . . sandbagging," said Storm. "Got it."

"Just let McQueen, Bobby Swift, and the others stay out front. Then pour it on in the final few laps. They won't know what hit 'em."

Storm took a deep breath. "I can't believe I finally made it here."

"Well, you better start believing! I already do. Now let's go *storm* that winner's circle!"

***

The first fifty laps were an utter mess. But that's normal for a rookie.

I must have said "Keep your cool!" twenty or thirty times into my headset.

Storm kept getting boxed in and squeezed out of every opportunity. Racers in a Piston Cup race are very aggressive, and the experience was different from anything he'd been through before. It was all I could do to keep him from ramming one of the other cars in frustration.

"They keep trash-talking me!" Storm shouted through my headset. "Someone just called me a poser!"

"Forget that and stay focused on the race," I said. "You need to start thinking about getting into position, like we planned."

And sure enough, slowly and methodically, Storm worked his way up. He was careful not to get ahead too much. By the time the pack of leaders had twenty laps remaining in the race, Storm was in the perfect position to do his work.

"Okay, okay!" I shouted into my headset as he blazed past my platform. "This is what you've been waiting for! It's time to step out of the shadows. GO, GO, GO!"

Without a word, Storm did what Storm does best: he began to zoom past the other racers as if they were standing still. I could hear his distinct engine howl above the roar of all the others.

On the next lap, Storm appeared cool and calm as he flashed by. From the subtle smile on his face, I could tell he was having the time of his life. On the other racers' faces, however, I caught looks of horror and disbelief as Storm moved past them with relentless efficiency.

I could feel the crowd's volume increase as they all started to ask, "Who is *that*?"

At some point, the roar of the spectators seemed to exceed the din of the racers. The entire stadium was electrified by the emergence of a surprise, come-from-behind contender.

I looked up at the stadium's jumbo screen as Storm surged past both McQueen and Swift. All the pain, all the practice, all the sacrifice, all the frustration was worth it for the absolute shock on McQueen's face.

Moments later, Storm flew across the finish line and the checkered flag finally waved.

The buzzing crowd exploded with excitement at the thrilling upset.

I was filled with pride. "YOU DID IT, STORM! YOU DID IT!" I screamed into my headset as Storm began his first victory lap.

"Thanks, Gus," he replied. "The Jackson Storm era has begun!"

It was the first time I'd heard him speak with pure joy in his voice. Things were shifting. Storm's future was bright—and the young racer was ready for it.

Cruz Ramirez is a young car with big dreams! She hopes one day to become a Piston Cup racer, like her hero Lightning McQueen. In the next *Cars Origins* adventure, join Cruz on her journey toward her destiny!

When I was young, I lived with my Aunt Carla and my two older cousins, Pablo and Victor. We didn't have much, but all we needed was each other. Aunt Carla was too busy working to pay us much mind, so we had lots of freedom. Maybe too much. We were noisy, rowdy, and competitive about absolutely everything, which entertained Aunt Carla to no end.

Our town's center was built around a boarded-up old tire factory. It was completely empty now, except for some old ad posters that were peeling from the walls. There were seventeen giant posters in all—each featuring a race car blazing around a track in the factory's tires. I memorized every one, studying all the details. Those posters were my gateway into a thrilling world that seemed light-years away from my small town. I used to daydream about what it would feel like to be on a real racetrack—hugging a turn, the wind against my face, going as fast as I dared alongside the other racers.

Aunt Carla liked to tell us about the old days when the tire factory was running at full steam. "The town actually had traffic back then, believe it or not," she said. When the factory closed, however, the town soon followed, as most of its residents moved out. Those who remained learned to live with less, and everybody focused on what was important: friends and family.

We lived in an old, empty muffler repair shop, which my family used to run, but when the town's fortunes took a downturn, so did our business. From the beginning, I just figured everybody lived in a closed-down shop, so it never occurred to me that we were struggling. And although we didn't have a lot, we were happy. Things weren't always easy, but I wouldn't have changed a thing.

The fourteen paved streets surrounding the old factory were still in pretty decent shape, since we were practically the only ones who used them. My cousins and I had memorized every curve, bump, and pothole. We'd race away the long summer days, constantly inventing new routes to keep things interesting.

"You're getting pretty fast, Cruz," my older cousin Pablo would tell me.

"No, you're just getting slower," I'd tease him.

Pablo was my hero. He loved to race more than anything else. He spoke fast, couldn't remain still, and yearned for adventure and excitement.

"There's a big world out there, Cruz," he told me more than once, "and I expect to race through most of it."

My cousin Victor was a bit younger than his brother Pablo. He was almost as fast as Pablo, but definitely not as reckless. Victor was the most sensible and responsible member of our family. He liked to say, "If common sense is so common, how come nobody seems to have any?"

Let's just say Pablo was a "gas tank half-full"

type of car, whereas Victor was a "gas tank half-empty" type. I loved them both equally.

My cousins were always trying to outrace me. They said girls couldn't keep up. That made me more determined than ever to prove them wrong. My goal was to race faster than both Pablo and Victor. I wanted to show them that girls could do anything they set their minds to. They could even race boys—and beat them!

We hung out at our town's one remaining attraction: a brushless car wash, which was also where Aunt Carla worked. We'd watch racing on the TV in the gift shop. That's where I first saw the car that would change the course of my life: Lightning McQueen.

That day the Racing Sports Network was covering Lightning at the Motor Speedway of the South. Even though he was just a rookie, Lightning stole the spotlight wherever he went. I watched wide-eyed as a reporter spoke with the red racer about competing in the biggest race of the Piston Cup season. He said he raced for the pure joy of moving fast, which I could relate to—I felt exactly the same way! But Lightning was so much cooler than I could ever be. He always had a confident, sly grin. And with the way he winked at the crowd and said that funny *"Ka-chow!"* thing, how could he not be the most popular racer on the track!

Once the green flag dropped, I couldn't take my eyes off Number 95. The race started off tight, but it didn't take long for Lightning to pull ahead. He lapped the other racers so many times, I lost count. Chick and The King were left in his dust. But then something unimaginable happened. One of Lightning's back tires blew! He swerved from side to side, struggling to maintain control. As he continued to race, his wheel sent up a shower of sparks. Moments later his second tire blew! I couldn't believe it! Chick and The King had caught up and were inches behind Lightning as he crawled toward the finish line. He extended his tongue for the craziest, most unbelievable photo finish ever!

Watching Lightning on TV that day changed something inside me. I knew what I was meant to do: race! If this rookie racer could make such an impact on the world of racing, who was to say I couldn't do the same thing?

That was when I made the announcement to my two cousins. "I'm going to be a famous race car one day, just like Lightning McQueen!"

"Go for it," said Pablo. "You just have to beat *me* first!"

Victor had a different response. "Dream small, Cruz," he said. "Dream small or not at all. Cars like us need to focus on one day at a time, not on big, fancy dreams for the future."

I didn't let Victor discourage me. I knew I was meant for something big and important. In my mind, I called it my "destination." I'd really meant "destiny," but I had the words mixed up. If you think about it, they're really two ways of saying the same thing. I told myself that as long as I was always driving toward my destination, I'd arrive there eventually, no matter how confused and loopy the route.

I also knew that this little spark of a dream, this flame of hope, would have to be protected. I'd have to be careful not to let anyone snuff it out. I'd let it grow secretly inside me. I understood that the more I talked about it, the more ridiculous I'd sound. I decided this was the type of thing that was best kept unsaid.

A few days after watching Lightning in that race, I rolled over to the old tire factory and examined the racing posters again. If I squinted just right, I could almost see myself up there, mouth creased in concentration, my tires gripping the hot asphalt, the crowd cheering my name: "Cruz! Cruz! Cruz!"

I wanted my own poster one day. I wanted to feel the rush of racing on a speedway. I wanted to be on TV, just like Lightning McQueen. But how you got from watching a race in a car wash gift shop to racing in the Piston Cup in front of millions was a complete mystery to me.

I just had to keep reminding myself that like anything else in life, if you're sure of the destination, you'll figure out along the way how to get there.

Continue to read about Cruz Ramirez in the next *Cars* Origins adventure!